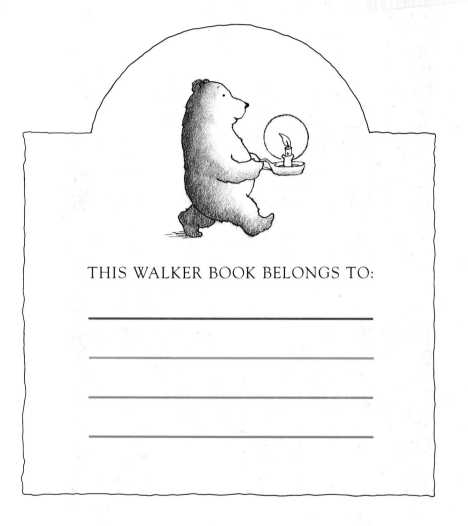

THIS WALKER BOOK BELONGS TO:

_____

_____

_____

_____

With special thanks to
Sam and his Grandad

First published 1989 by Walker Books Ltd
87 Vauxhall Walk, London SE11 5HJ

This edition published 2002

2 4 6 8 10 9 7 5 3 1

© 1989 Blackbird Design Pty Ltd

The right of Bob Graham to be identified as author
of this work has been asserted by him in accordance with
the Copyright, Designs and Patents Act 1988

This book has been typeset in Times

Printed in China

British Library Cataloguing in Publication Data:
a catalogue record for this book is available from the British Library

ISBN 0-7445-8916-9

Grandad's MaGiC

BOB GRAHAM

WALKER BOOKS

AND SUBSIDIARIES

LONDON · BOSTON · SYDNEY

Three dogs lived in Alison's house.

Two sat high on the shelf. They were very precious
to Alison's mum. They were very breakable.

Alison was not to touch them even if she could reach.
She didn't like them anyway.

Alison much preferred Rupert. He lived on the armchair.

Rupert only left the chair to have his dinner or go
to the toilet.

He wouldn't leave the chair for Alison's mum *or* her dad, and certainly not for Max, who often tried to pull his tail.

Rupert wouldn't even get out of his chair when Grandma and Grandad came to lunch on Sunday.

Alison held Max for Grandma
to kiss. He curled his fists and
kicked his legs.

"Give him to me," said Grandad.
"I know how to handle this young chap.
Now for my magic . . ."

Grandad reached into Max's shirt and slowly pulled out a chocolate bear. "Have you been keeping that in your shirt all this time?" he said.

Max's face lit up with pleasure.

Then Grandad lost the bear . . .

and found it again under Rupert's collar!
"It's magic," said Alison.

"Watch me, Grandad," said Alison.

She had a trick of her own. She was learning to juggle with three puffins filled with sand that Grandad had given her.

This *sounded* easy, but she had to keep them going from hand to hand. The idea was to have three puffins in the air all at once.

"Try one at a time, Alison," said Grandad. "Backwards and forwards . . .

and when you learn that, try two, and when you learn that, try three."

"I'm not as good as I used to be," said Grandad.

Sunday was the only day the china dogs came down from
the shelf. Alison's mum used them as a table decoration.
They guarded the fruit.

Every Sunday Grandad picked his table napkin out of the air like an apple off a tree.

And he talked of his best trick of all . . .

"I used to be able to take this tablecloth, give it a
pull in a certain kind of way, and it would whip out from
under all this stuff and leave everything standing there.

But that was a long time ago."

Then one Sunday,
Grandad noticed
how well Alison
juggled, and...

without warning, he removed his coat and climbed
on to the chair.

"One good trick deserves another," he said.
And he gave the tablecloth a short, snapping tug.

There was a moment of silence. Mum looked pale.
"You did it!" said Alison.
Grandad did a triumphant dance round the room.
And *that's* when it happened.

An orange rolled off the bowl, hit one of the precious dogs and sent it spinning into mid-air . . .

just as Rupert happened to be making a trip to the toilet.

It settled on his very broad back . . .

then landed safely in Max's lap.

Alison held her breath. Would Grandad get into trouble?

But Mum smiled thinly as she put the dogs back on the shelf.
"Don't *you* try that trick, Ally," said Grandad.

The following Sunday there were a number of changes in
Alison's house. When Grandma and Grandad came to lunch,

the dogs stayed on the shelf.

And the table was set with unbreakable plastic plates and place mats.

Just before lunch, Rupert found a box of chocolates hidden under his cushion.

Later, Grandad made the chocolates appear just like magic.
They were for Mum, who had such a shock last week.

Alison was dismayed.
"That's not magic, it's a trick!

You put them there, Grandad.
The price is still on them!"

"We performers can't get it right all the time, Alison," Grandad said, "but the chocolates have certainly vanished."

"Now, let's see how long *you* can spin this plastic plate on the end of your finger!"

BOB GRAHAM is a leading
contemporary picture-book maker.
He has written and illustrated many children's
picture books for Walker, including *Brand New Baby*;
Rose Meets Mr Wintergarten; *Queenie the Bantam*
(Highly Commended for the Kate Greenaway Medal);
Buffy (Smarties Book Prize Silver Award Winner);
Max (Winner of the 2000 Smarties Gold Medal);
Let's Get a Pup; and *Jethro Byrde, Fairy Child*.
He also illustrated *This Is Our House*, written by
Michael Rosen. Having lived in Britain for many years,
he recently moved back to his native Australia.